Picture Book of Classica...

中国传统故事美绘本（中英文双语版）

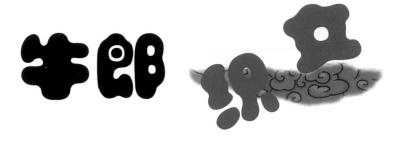

Niulang and Zhinü

很早以前，在南阳城西的牛家庄，住着一个勤劳善良的小伙子，人们都叫他牛郎。牛郎父母早亡，只好跟哥嫂一起生活。嫂嫂为人十分刻薄。牛郎每天天没亮就起床，忙到天黑了才回家，尽管这样，嫂嫂也经常吹毛求疵，还动不动就找茬骂他一顿。幸亏牛郎是个忠厚老实的孩子，只管干自己的活儿，不跟嫂嫂一般计较。

A long time ago, in a village lying west in Nanyang, there lived a good natured boy named Niulang (literally "cowherd"). Niulang's parents passed away when he was young, leaving him to live with his brother and sister-in-law. His sister-in-law was very hard on him. Niulang woke up at dawn every day and worked till the sun went down, but even so, his sister-in-law was never satisfied. Often, she would yell at Niulang and scold him for being lazy. But Niulang was a kind-hearted and loyal boy and never fought back.

眼看牛郎就十五岁了，快到成家立业的时候了。嫂嫂心里打起了小算盘。家里的房子、田地都是牛郎兄弟的父母留下来的，万一牛郎哪天提出来分割家产就麻烦了。于是，嫂嫂找来牛郎，对他说："牛郎啊，父母去世得早，记得当时你才八岁。经过这么多年，我们终于把你拉扯大啦。"牛郎一听嫂嫂谈起父母，不禁心酸得流下了泪水。嫂嫂接着说道："你现在长大了，咱们也该分家了。我们家最值钱的莫过于那头耕牛了，人们不是常说嘛，牛是农家宝，种田少不了。你就带着那头耕牛离开吧。其他的不值钱的东西，都归我们。"

　　Time passed, and Niulang was soon to turn fifteen, of an age to think about marriage and a career. His sister-in-law began to worry about the division of their porperty. The house and the fields had all been left to Niulang and his brother when their parents passed away. In the event that Niulang started asking questions about the will, his sister-in-law was sure to be in trouble. So she went to Niulang and said, "Niulang, your parents passed away when you were so young. You were only eight years old. Now we have finally raised you to be a grown man." Her mention of his parents brought tears to Niulang's eyes, but she continued, "Now that you are older, it is time to split up the assets so that you can have a bright future. The one thing we have that is of any value is our ox. Don't they always say, 'The ox is the treasure of the farm; with it your crops will always be bountiful?' So take the ox, Niulang. As for the rest which worthless, we'll keep it."

牛郎心里明白,嫂嫂是迫不及待地想将他赶出门呢。嫂嫂说的最值钱的那头耕牛,是一头老牛。这头牛实在是太老啦,牙都掉光了,耕一圈地,得呼哧呼哧喘半天气。在嫂嫂眼里,这头牛是干不了什么活了。但在牛郎眼里,这头老牛是他最好的朋友。

　　自从父母去世后,是这头老牛陪伴牛郎度过了最寂寞的时光。每天,牛郎都会对着老牛述说自己的喜怒哀乐。老牛似乎能听懂牛郎的话。牛郎难过的时候,老牛也难过;牛郎开心的时候,老牛也开心。"不管怎么说,幸亏,至少,老牛我能带走。"牛郎这么想着,便说道:"好吧,嫂嫂。"嫂嫂听了心花怒放。

Niulang knew that his sister-in-law could not wait to drive him from the door. The ox that she described as their most valuable asset was actually very old—so old that its teeth were falling out. Even one trip around the field left it breathless. In the sister-in-law's eyes, the animal was basically useless. But in Niulang's eyes, this ox was a treasured friend.

After his parents had passed away, it was this ox that had stayed by him through all the lonely times. Every day Niulang would talk to the ox, telling his woes and joys. The ox seemed to understand him better than anyone else in the world. When Niulang was sad, so was the ox. When Niulang was happy, so was the ox. "In spite of everything, at least I am lucky enough to have the ox with me," Niulang thought. So he said to his sister-in-law, "Okay then." She was overjoyed by what she took for his simple-minded assent.

牛郎牵了老牛出来，头也不回地往山里走去。他一直走啊走啊，也不知走了多久，来到了一处有着青山绿水的地方，牛郎打算就把家安在这里。从此，牛郎和老牛相依为命。他们在山上披荆斩棘，耕田种地，盖造房屋。一年后，营造了一个小小的家，能够勉强度日。就是家里实在是太冷清了。每天牛郎依旧会对着这头不会说话的老牛说话，但老牛真的是越来越老啦。

Niulang and his ox left the village and walked towards the mountains without even a backwards glance. They walked and walked, and after a long time they arrived at a beautiful place with green mountains and clear waters. Niulang decided that this would be the site of his new home. From then on, Niulang and his ox had only each other to rely on. They cleared new land, worked in the field and started to build a new house. A year later, they had successfully fashioned a new home for themselves. However, it was a lonely life Niulang was leading, his only companion being an ox who could not speak back to him. And his companion was getting older by the day.

这天，牛郎在外面打好一筐嫩青草，来喂老牛。老牛突然开口说话了，把牛郎吓了一大跳。老牛对他说："你今天下午去碧莲池一趟，有几个仙女会在水里嬉戏。你将那件红色的外衣藏起来，那件衣服的主人就会成为你的妻子。""真的吗，牛大哥？"牛郎又奇怪又高兴。老牛点了点头。

One day, just as Niulang had finished gathering some fresh grass to feed his ox, suddenly the animal spoke, scaring Niulang half to death. "Go to Bilian Pond today; there will be fairies there playing in the water. Take the red dress and hide it well. The owner of that dress will be your wife."

"Really, Brother Ox?" Niulang was both excited and hesitant. The old ox nodded.

牛郎于是就悄悄藏在碧莲池边的芦苇丛里。果然，不一会儿，仙女们飘然而至，脱下外衣跃入池中玩耍。牛郎从芦苇丛里跑出来，拿了那件红色外衣就躲到了一边。仙女们一见有人来了，慌忙从水里跑出来披上外衣，个个像受惊的小鸟一样嗖的飞上天空，转眼就不见了。只剩下最后一个仙女在那里正着急，她的红色外衣找不到了，没有外衣，就没法飞上天去。牛郎于是捧着衣服走出来，对这位仙女说："你要是答应做我的妻子，我就把衣服还给你。"

Niulang made his way down to the pond and hid in a dense reeds nearby. After a short time, fairies indeed appeared and took off their dresses before plunging into the pond. Niulang quietly approached, snatched the red dress and hid. Sensing that someone was near, all the fairies jumped out of the pond and hurriedly donned their clothes. They quickly took flight and made their way up to the heavens. Only one fairy was left, panicking as she looked for her red dress. Without it she could not return to the heavens. Niulang came out from his hiding place and said, "If you promise to become my wife, I will give you back your dress."

原来，这位仙女名叫织女，是王母娘娘的孙女，在天上专管织云彩。织女的手很巧，织的云彩不仅色彩绚丽无比，而且形态各异，将天空打扮得异常美丽。

早上，当太阳刚刚打着哈欠从海边露出脸庞的时候，织女织出粉色、红色、玫瑰色的彩云，衬托太阳红红的脸蛋；下午，天空湛蓝无比，织女就织出洁白的云朵，再将这些云朵捏成各种形状，有奔腾的骏马，温顺的绵羊，盛开的鲜花，飞舞的飘带等，来点缀蓝天；到了傍晚，织女又织出金色的彩带给一片片云彩镶上漂亮的金边……

牛郎也向织女述说了自己的身世，告诉她这次是老牛安排他在这里等着她。织女听了，不禁对眼前的这个小伙子生了爱慕之心。

This fairy's name was Zhinü (literally "weaver girl"). She was the granddaughter of the Queen Mother of the West and was responsible for weaving the clouds in the sky. Zhinü had gifted hands; her clouds were radiant and breathtaking. She made the world a more beautiful place.

In the morning, Zhinü would weave pink, red and rosy clouds to accompany the sunrise; in the afternoon, when the sky was clear and blue, she would weave puffs of clouds of all shapes and sizes, such as galloping horses, sweet lambs, blossoming flowers and dancing ribbons; at dusk, she would fashion golden ribbons as a decorative border to all the wonderful clouds.

Niulang told Zhinü of his past and of his ox's plan for him to meet her. Hearing his story, Zhinü began to fall in love with this kind, orphaned boy.

两人结婚后，男耕女织，相亲相爱，日子过得非常美满幸福。不久，他们就生下一双可爱的儿女，一家人过得其乐融融。但好景不长，织女私自下凡与凡人成婚的事被王母娘娘知道了，她非常恼怒，发誓要拆散牛郎织女。

而正在这个时候，牛郎家的那头老牛死了。牛郎哭得十分伤心。按照老牛临死前的嘱托，牛郎将它身上的牛皮剥下来放好，然后好好埋葬了老牛。

The two were married and led a simple and happy life together. Not long after, Zhinü gave birth to a baby girl and a boy and, for a time, their family lived together harmoniously and happily. However their happiness did not last long. Soon after, the Queen Mother of the West found out about her granddaughter living in the mortal world with her husband. She was very angry and vowed to separate them.

It was at this time that Niulang's old ox passed away. Heartbroken Niulang couldn't help crying. He then stripped the ox of his hide, as the ox had instructed before his death, and buried his loyal friend.

这天，牛郎下地干活，剩下织女和两个孩子在家。突然间狂风大作，几个天兵从天而降，不由分说，押起织女就飞上天。牛郎觉得不对劲，跑回家一看，家里只剩下孩子们正大哭着叫妈妈。眼见织女被天兵押着越飞越高，牛郎急得不知如何是好。这时，他突然想起老牛临终前嘱咐他，牛皮在关键的时候可以拿出来救急。于是牛郎便赶紧将两个孩子放在两个箩筐里，披上牛皮，挑起箩筐，牛皮就带着他们向天空飞去。

Later Niulang left the house to go to work in the field, leaving Zhinü and their children at home. Suddenly, the sky clouded over and several soldiers swooped down from the heavens and took Zhinü away. Niulang, realizing that something was wrong, raced back home, but he was too late. All that was left were his two crying children. He looked up and saw his lovely wife being dragged back to the skies. Feeling completely helpless as he watched his wife getting farther and farther away, Niulang suddenly remembered that his old ox had instructed him that his hide could be used in times of great emergency. He quickly put his two children in baskets, carried them on a shoulder pole, and threw on the ox hide as it began to ascend. Soon he was flying towards the skies.

织女正哭得肝肠寸断，被押着往天上飞，忽然听到后面传来了牛郎的叫声："织女，等等我！"织女回头一看，只见牛郎披着牛皮，挑着一双儿女正往这边追过来呢。织女又惊又喜，眼泪不住地流。孩子们看到妈妈，都张开双臂，大叫："妈妈！妈妈！"眼看就要追上了，王母娘娘架着云飞过来，拔下头上的金簪，在他们中间一划。刹那间，一条波涛滚滚的天河挡住了牛郎的去路。

Zhinü was sobbing pitifully as her captors carried her farther and farther up into the skies. Then, suddenly, she heard Niulang's voice behind her, "Zhinü, wait for me!" Zhinü looked back and saw her dear husband and children flying after her in an ox hide. Zhinü was both surprised and excited, and her tears flowed endlessly as her children held out their arms crying, "Mama! Mama!" Just as they were about to catch up, the Queen Mother appeared in a cloud and slashed the air with her golden hairpin, creating the Milky Way in the sky, thus separating the lovers.

从此，牛郎和织女就在天河两岸，互相守望，相对哭泣，不愿离去。他们忠贞的爱情感动了喜鹊。千万只喜鹊搭成鹊桥，让牛郎织女走上鹊桥相会。王母娘娘一看也无奈，只好允许两人在每年的农历七月七日于鹊桥相会。

　　后来，每到农历七月初七，相传牛郎织女鹊桥相会的日子，姑娘们就会来到花前月下，抬头仰望星空，寻找银河两边的牛郎星和织女星。她们希望能看到他们一年一度的相会，并祈祷自己能有称心美满的婚姻。这一天也成为了中国的"情人节"。

Ever since then, the two lovers have been trapped on either side of the Milky Way. They can only look at one another from afar, crying since neither has the heart to leave the Milky Way. Moved by their love, the magpies in the sky joined together to form a bridge across the starry expanse with their bodies. The Queen Mother allows the magpies to do this only once a year, on the 7th day of the 7th lunar month.

That is why, on the 7th day of the 7th lunar month of every year, girls from all over will gather under the moon and look up to see Niulang and Zhinü come together. They hope that they too will be lucky enough to find a husband who loves them so truly and deeply. This day has come to be the Chinese Valentine's Day.

完

End